DICK KING-SMITH COLLECTION

E.S.P

HORSE PIE

THE GUARD DOG

YOUNG CORGI BOOKS

DICK KING-SMITH COLLECTION
A YOUNG CORGI BOOK : 0 552 54610 0

First published in Great Britain

PRINTING HISTORY
This collection first published 1998

5 7 9 10 8 6 4

Cover artwork by Peter Wingham

including:
E.S.P.
First published in Great Britain in 1986 by
Marilyn Malin Books in association with Andre Deutsch Ltd
Based on original design by Belitha Press
Young Corgi edition published 1989
Reissued 1998

HORSE PIE
First published in Great Britain in 1993 by
Doubleday, a division of Transworld Publishers Ltd
Young Corgi edition published 1994

THE GUARD DOG
First published in Great Britain in 1991 by
Doubleday, a division of Transworld Publishers Ltd
Young Corgi edition published 1992

Corgi Books are published by Transworld Publishers,
61–63 Uxbridge Road, London W5 5SA,
a division of The Random House Group Ltd,
in Australia by Random House Australia (Pty) Ltd,
20 Alfred Street, Milsons Point, Sydney, NSW 2061, Australia,
in New Zealand by Random House New Zealand Ltd,
18 Poland Road, Glenfield, Auckland 10, New Zealand
and in South Africa by Random House (Pty) Ltd,
Endulini, 5a Jubilee Road, Parktown 2193, South Africa

Printed and bound in Great Britain by
Cox & Wyman Ltd, Reading, Berkshire.

Rory MD

E.S.P.

DICK KING-SMITH

Illustrated by Peter Wingham

YOUNG CORGI BOOKS

1. *Redcar*

Eric Stanley Pigeon was born above a newsagent's shop. Quite high above, in fact. On the roof. He was born in a nest in a gulley between a skylight and a chimney-pot.

Because he was Mr and Mrs Pigeon's first baby, there was some discussion about what they should call him. Mr Pigeon rather fancied 'Walter', but Mrs Pigeon said 'Pooh-pooh!' to this and reeled off a selection of names of her own choice. To each of these Mr Pigeon merely remarked 'Coo!' In the end it was decided (Mrs Pigeon decided) that the child should be named Eric (after Mr Pigeon) and Stanley (after a favourite great-uncle).

When Eric Stanley Pigeon's eyes opened, the first thing upon which they focused was a sheet of newspaper. Mrs Pigeon had not bothered with much of a nest, but she had decorated the site with a few oddments picked up

from the pavement below – a cigarette packet, some milk-bottle tops, a sweet-wrapper and the piece of newspaper. Thus it was that Eric Stanley Pigeon's first experience of the printed word came in the shape of the racing page of *The Daily Echo*, informing him of the runners and riders for the meetings at Redcar and Uttoxeter, six weeks earlier.

Something about the lists of horses seemed to attract Eric

Stanley Pigeon, and he began to peck vigorously at one particular name.

'Leave that alone, Eric Stanley!' said Mrs Pigeon sharply. 'You don't know where it's been.'

There is no telling whether Eric Stanley Pigeon would have obeyed his mother, for at that moment a gust of wind came swooping across the roof-tops and caught the sheet, sending it twirling away. It floated across the street below, and over a wall

into what was locally known as 'The Park'.

The Park was an area of dirty grass and dusty trees, with a few swings and a seesaw in one corner, and a couple of benches that

had long forgotten the feel of a lick of paint. On one of these benches there sat a tramp.

For the tramp, the Park was home, and there he was a familiar figure, known to all (with good

reason) as Old Smelly. With a last tired flap, the racing page of *The Daily Echo* landed in his lap.

Newspapers were very important to Old Smelly. Sometimes the newsagent would let him have the odd unsold copy from the previous day but mostly he relied on finding discarded papers that people had read and dropped into rubbish bins. He collected them in a sack. He needed them, not primarily to read, but to cover himself at night. Others might sleep under sheets and blankets or duvets, but Old Smelly slept under a thick layer of newspapers. The only parts of them that he did read were the racing pages, for Old Smelly was a gambler. Backing horses was what had brought him to his present state, and even now, when he had no money to lose, the subject was of absorbing interest to him.

He smoothed out the page that had come from Eric Stanley's nest and ran his eye down it. There was a mark, he noticed, against the name of one of the runners in the 2.30 at Redcar, a small hole in the paper, as though someone had stuck a pin in it. Lucky Choice, the horse was called. He looked at the date on top of the page. March 5th.

Old Smelly sat in the April sunshine and was suddenly curious to know if the choice had been lucky. He reached into his old sack, and after a good deal of

searching found a copy of *The Daily Echo* for March 6th. He turned to 'Yesterday's Racing Results'.

'Redcar. 2.30. 2 Mile Handicap Hurdle,' he read. '*1. Lucky*

Choice. 10–1.' Nice odds, thought Old Smelly. I wish I could pick 'em like that.

2. Newmarket

Halfway through May, Eric Stanley Pigeon made his maiden flight. For some time he had been practising beating his wings up and down, and one day it was plain to his parents that he would soon be leaving home. This, they agreed privately, would be a relief, for he took a great deal of feeding. But they considered it their duty to prepare him for the wide world beyond the roof of the newsagent's shop.

'Now humans are generally all right,' said Mrs Pigeon, 'the big ones anyway – the little ones might chuck things at you – but don't trust their dogs, Eric Stanley, d'you hear me?'

'Dogs! Coo!' said Mr Pigeon.

'And, specially, watch out for cats.'

'Cats! Coo-er!' said Mr Pigeon.

'And I shouldn't go too far to start with,' said Mrs Pigeon. 'Just as far as the Park. There are no cars in there, or nasty motorbikes.'

'Vroom-vroom-vroom!' said Mr Pigeon loudly.

So when the moment came, that's where Eric Stanley Pigeon went.

In the middle of a training

session, the wind once more sneaked over the roof-tops and lifted Eric Stanley off the nest and over the edge of the roof. Flapping madly, he cleared the busy noisy street beneath, and saw below him an open grassy space. Here he landed, rather too fast, so that he tipped forward on to his beak. Recovering his balance, Eric Stanley Pigeon looked up to find himself staring at a large pair of boots, out of the toecaps of which peeped some filthy toes.

'Hullo, young feller-me-lad!' said a voice. 'Crash-landing that were, if ever I seen one. You wants to get your under-carriage down a bit smarter.'

Coo! thought Eric Stanley, this

must be a human, and a big one too. Well, Mum said they were O.K.

He ran his gaze upwards, from the battered boots to the torn trousers to the old overcoat, and finally to the face that was peering down at him, a face that was covered in a great matted bush of hair. Funny-looking things, humans, thought Eric Stanley. At that moment a piece of bread was dropped in front of him.

Old Smelly had had a particularly good morning. The greengrocer had given him a couple of bruised apples and a handful of carrots out of the box marked 'For Rabbits', the girl in the baker's shop had slipped him a whole stale loaf, and at the newsagent's they had let him have a copy of one of the previous day's unsold newspapers. He had been reading this – the racing pages – when Eric Stanley arrived, and now laid it down open on the bench beside him.

'Was that nice, young feller?' said Old Smelly. 'Have a bit more,' and he crumbled some more bread over the paper.

'Jump up here,' he said. 'I shan't hurt you.'

The noises the human was making meant nothing to Eric Stanley, but the bread had tasted good, so he did as he was bid. Like most birds, he had no sense of smell, so that getting close to the tramp did not worry him as it would have worried another human, and he gobbled up the crumbs eagerly. Then, it seemed, something on the printed page caught his attention and he began to peck again, not at the bread but at the paper itself, at one particular place. He pecked in fact until his beak made a small hole in the page. Then he flew away.

Old Smelly put the rest of the loaf back in his filthy pocket and picked up his paper again. He looked at the little hole that the young pigeon had made at the end of a line. He ran his filthy finger-nail along the line, which gave details of a horse entered in the 4.10 race at yesterday's Newmarket meeting. Jamonit was the animal's name.

Old Smelly scratched his filthy head with his filthy finger-nail, stuffed the newspaper into his other filthy pocket along with the apples and the rabbit-carrots, and made off across the Park towards the betting-shop.

The betting-shop manager was not keen on having Old Smelly in his shop – it was bad for custom – but the tramp's luck held. The manager was busy and did not see him as he slipped in and stood before the pinned-up lists of yesterday's racing results.

'*Newmarket. 4.10,*' read Old Smelly. '*1. Jamonit. 12–1.*'

Back on his bench, Old Smelly sat deep in thought. Then he gave voice to his thoughts, to an audience of sparrows.

'That bird,' said Old Smelly, 'picked a winner. Or I should say, he pecked a winner. By making a hole. Just like that hole I found the other day – at Redcar,

wasn't it. Lucky Choice, that was it. You don't suppose, do you, that that bird could have . . . known?'

The sparrows all cheeped loudly, but whether in agreement

or not Old Smelly could not tell. He shook his head and grinned to himself under his filthy beard.

'What rubbish!' he said to the sparrows. 'I must be going bonkers. Why, to do that, that bird would have to have, what do they call it – Extra Sensory Perception, that's it. E.S.P.!'

3. *Newbury*

Eric Stanley Pigeon flew gaily over the Park the following morning. He had now gone solo for a good many hours and had mastered the art of flight and its necessary accompaniments, take-off and landing. He landed now, in one of the dusty trees, and looked down at the scene below.

The human was sitting, as usual, on his bench. At his feet there strutted and bobbed and cooed a whole crowd of pigeons, including Eric Stanley's parents.

'How in the world am I going to be able to tell you apart from the rest?' said Old Smelly to the bluey-grey look-alike throng, as yet another flew down from the tree above to join it. As if to

answer his question this last bird flapped up on to the bench beside him.

'Eric Stanley!' called Mrs Pigeon sharply. 'Come down off there at once, d'you hear me?' But just then Old Smelly reached under the bench for his sack. At the movement all the birds on the ground flew away. The tramp studied the remaining pigeon. Then he took out an old newspaper and opened it, carefully, at the 'Today's Radio and Television' page.

Eric Stanley made no move.

Gently, slowly, Old Smelly turned the sheets until he reached the racing pages. Immediately the pigeon walked on to the paper and began to peck. Peck, peck, peck, peck he went, at the one spot, until a little hole appeared beside the name of a horse.

The tramp did not bother to look at it, or at the date of the old yellowing newspaper.

'Whatever nag that was, my

lad,' he said to the bird, 'one thing's certain. It was first past the post next day. You're my boy all right, you're the one with the Extra Sensory Perception. I think I'll call you E.S.P. Makes a nice name for you. Now then, E.S.P., what we gotta do is get hold of a copy of today's paper. Then you can peck me a horse and I'll be off to the betting-shop at full gallop. Talk about putting money on a stone-cold certainty! Only trouble is, though, I ain't even got the money for a paper. What we going to do, E.S.P.?'

'Coo,' said Eric Stanley. He was thinking about food.

Whether Old Smelly begged, borrowed or stole a copy of that day's *Daily Echo*, Eric Stanley neither knew nor cared, but when he flew back later to the bench after a few tours of the Park, he found the paper there, spread open at the proper place. More important to Eric Stanley, the tramp gave him his last bit of bread.

There were three race meetings that day. Eric Stanley showed no interest in Thirsk or Market Rasen, but walked straight to the list of runners at Newbury and began to peck at a point in the

4.30 until that little hole appeared.

'Here, shift over, E.S.P.,' said Old Smelly. 'Let's have a dekko. Nice Surprise, is it? Never heard of him but it will be, for sure. If I only had the lolly.'

Eric Stanley, having pecked his horse, was not interested in all the noises the human made, and he had strutted off down the tarmac path, investigating, as pigeons do, anything and everything on the ground. Like most places in the Park, it was thick with rubbish. Beer-can tops, spent matches, old ice-cream tubs – all were examined by young Eric Stanley in his search for something to eat; and then suddenly his eye was caught, on that bright warm morning, by a smallish round object. The sun glinted on its flat surface.

He picked it up in his beak to see if it was edible. Finding that it wasn't, he dropped it. It tinkled. Eric Stanley rather liked the noise it made, and he walked back towards the bench, picking up this new toy and dropping it again. He dropped it, eventually, at Old Smelly's smelly old feet.

There was too much hair on

the tramp's face for Eric Stanley to see that he turned quite pale. He bent over, stroking the pigeon with one hand. With the other, he picked up the pound coin.

'What a bird!' said Old Smelly in a kind of hoarse whisper. 'What a bird you are, E.S.P.! First you pecks the winner. Then you pecks up the stake money. We're in business, all thanks to you, young feller-me-lad, and I shan't forget what you done for me.'

Old Smelly went into the betting-shop with the pound coin gripped tightly in his hand (for all his pockets were full of was holes). He wrote out a betting-slip, and took it to the counter.

Wrinkling his nose in distaste, the manager picked up the slip between finger and thumb, and looked suspiciously at the coin.

'Where d'you get that from?' he said sourly.

'Friend give it to me,' said Old Smelly.

A picture of E.S.P. in flight came into his mind, and he grinned behind his whiskers.

STORES
SALE
SALE

'I'm putting it on for him,' he said. 'He felt like having a flutter.'

4. *Epsom*

Old Smelly waited happily in the sunshine outside the betting-shop until the results of the 4.30 at Newbury came in. Nice Surprise had won easily.

'Your friend's lucky,' said the

manager as he handed over the winnings. 'Twenty quid and more he's won. Let's hope he gives you a bit for your trouble. You could get yourself smartened up.'

Even Eric Stanley, with his very limited knowledge of humans, could see the difference in his friend, when he flew down to the bench next morning. To begin with, he couldn't see Old Smelly's toes. Gone were the broken boots and instead he was wearing a pair of wellies. Gone were the torn trousers and the old overcoat, to be replaced by a rather shiny second-hand blue suit. Gone were quite a lot of the whiskers, for the tramp had had his beard trimmed. Into the hole in it in which his lips were now visible he was thrusting a large piece of fresh bread, followed by a large lump of Cheddar cheese.

'Hullo, E.S.P.!' said Old Smelly with his mouth full. 'Come here, my son. I got something for you,' and he tipped out, on to a crisp copy of a newly-printed *Daily Echo*, a handful of chocolate drops. 'Got 'em in the newsagent's,' he said.

'Special for you. And I've still got a fiver left. For today.'

He waited till Eric Stanley had picked up the chocolate drops, and then opened the paper.

'Now then,' he said, 'what's it to be?'

It was to be a horse called Three Loud Cheers, which that afternoon won at 8–1, and turned Old Smelly's fiver into forty pounds. And each day that week, Eric Stanley pecked the tramp a winner.

Old Smelly did not use all his winnings for each day's bet. Though he continued to sleep in the Park under his blanket of old newspapers and did not allow soap and water to touch his flesh, he did buy quite a few luxuries, mainly in the way of food, and he always gave Eric Stanley a generous share. Nevertheless, all the time his winnings were growing, and so was an idea in his mind.

Like all gamblers, he had

ESP 1

always dreamed of one really enormous win, a win that would set him up for the rest of his life. Now, for the first time, he had enough money to make that dream come true. E.S.P. would choose the right horse. All he had to do was to put everything that he had won on it.

As May drew to a close, Old Smelly made up his mind to act. For one thing, he knew he could not count on E.S.P.'s help for ever. The bird might get killed, by a cat or a car, or it might just fly away and never come back. And for another thing, the following Wednesday, the first one in June, was Derby Day.

The notion of having a fantastically colossal win on the Derby tickled Old Smelly's fancy.

When he bought his *Daily Echo* on Derby Day, the entire centre spread of it was taken up with the great race – a picture of the favourite, a map of the course, the tipsters' selections, and the list of runners and riders. He spread it out on the bench and waited. Before long there came a whistle of wings and a bluey-grey figure landed beside him.

To a pigeon's eye (Mrs Pigeon's for example) there was a certain obvious difference of appearance between Eric Stanley and his father. To a human eye there was absolutely none. Recently Eric Stanley had been telling his parents of the excellent grub that

his human friend was providing, like chocolate drops and other sweets, and potato crisps, and biscuits, all of which the tramp bought at the newsagent's, to share between them.

'Coo-er!' said Mr Pigeon, and he secretly determined to muscle in on his son's racket.

Now he stood on the bench and waited, impatiently, while the human made noises.

'Now then, E.S.P.,' said Old Smelly. 'You listen to me. This is the big one. It's the Derby, see, and once you've pecked me the winner I'm going to stick the whole lot on it, every penny I've got, what you've won for me, all five hundred quid of it. So get on with it, there's a clever lad, and if it's a long-priced outsider I shan't object one little bit.'

He took out a tube of Smarties and emptied a handful on to the centre spread.

Mr Pigeon had never come across Smarties before, and he found that they spurted away like tiddleywinks as he struck at them, causing him to pierce a number of holes in the paper in his efforts to nail them.

'Hurry up. Don't mess about,'

said Old Smelly, and when the bird had flown away he looked eagerly to see what choice it had made. Strangely, this time there were quite a few holes, in the picture of the favourite, in the map of the course, and in the tipsters' selections. But there was only one that mattered to him, the one that was in the right place, in the list of runners.

There it was, right bang in the middle of a horse's name. Some Hope.

Hastily Old Smelly looked at the odds.

Some Hope. 100–1 against!

Blimey, he thought, a hundred to one outsider is going to

win the Derby today! And I'm going to put £500 on it!! And that means I'm going to win £50,000!!! All because a little bird told me.

When Eric Stanley arrived at the bench later, it was empty, except for the newspaper. Out of habit now, he walked on to it and made yet one more hole in it, with a series of firm pecks against The Real McCoy, second favourite at 3–1. Then he flew off, and before long the wind took the paper and whirled it away to join the rest of the litter in the Park.

Old Smelly did not return to his bench till late afternoon. He slumped down and buried his head in his hands, the very

picture of dejection. He did not even move when Eric Stanley landed beside him, having missed his usual treats at breakfast and lunch and trusting to better luck at tea-time.

Eric Stanley pecked hopefully at the shiny blue sleeve of the tramp's jacket. Old Smelly looked up wearily.

'You let me down,' he said sadly. 'You let me down, E.S.P. A horse called The Real McCoy won the Derby. As for the one you pecked for me – you want to know where he came in? Last. Last of all, Some Hope was. The rest was gone home to tea when he finished. I tell you straight, I shan't never trust you to peck a horse no more. Never. You and your Extra Sensory Perception. And I tell you something else, I shan't never bet no more neither. It's a mug's game. Look!' and he turned his pockets inside out.

They were empty except for a betting-slip and the Smartie

tube. Slowly, deliberately, the tramp tore the betting-slip in half and tossed the pieces over his shoulder. Then he emptied the Smartie tube into the palm of his filthy hand. There were only a couple left. He sighed. Then, gradually, a smile spread over his hairy face.

'I ain't got no money,' he said, 'but I suppose at least I've got a friend,' and he gave one of his last two Smarties to the bird.

'Coo,' said Eric Stanley.

Old Smelly stroked the shining bluey-grey feathers.

'Some Hope,' he said ruefully. 'At 100–1. And I goes and puts five hundred quid on the thing. I needs my head examined.'

'Too true,' said Eric Stanley Pigeon (or that's what it sounded like to the tramp), 'too true,' and he flew up into the clean blue sky above the dirty Park.

Old Smelly watched the pigeon climbing.

'There's one thing certain, my boy,' he shouted after him. 'All this "E.S.P." business is a load of rubbish!'

THE END

HORSE PIE

DICK KING-SMITH

ILLUSTRATED BY VALERIE LITTLEWOOD

YOUNG CORGI BOOKS

HORSE PIE

Chapter One

"She'll have to go," said the donkeyman.

"Who?" said his son, Sam.

"Old Jenny. She's got so slow. Didn't you see that kid just now trying to make her walk a bit faster? She was miles behind the others. She's past it."

Sam squiggled sand between his

bare toes as he looked at the line of donkeys, waiting patiently for their next riders.

"What will happen to her, Dad?" he said.

"Have to see if they've got room for her at the Donkey Sanctuary," said his father.

"And if they haven't?"

"Cats' meat, I'm afraid," said the donkeyman.

"You mean . . .?"

"Yes. Have to send the old girl to the slaughterhouse."

"Oh, Dad, you couldn't! Not old Jenny!" Sam pleaded.

"Well, you think of a better idea then."

"Have a look at this," said the

Manager of the Old Horses' Home to his stableman, a couple of days later.

"What is it, boss?"

"Letter from a kid. Son of the chap that keeps the beach donkeys at Easton-super-Mare."

The stableman read the letter.

" '. . . Donkey Sanctuary full up . . . slaughterhouse . . . you are her last hope . . . Please, please!' Oh dear, pulls at your heart-strings, doesn't it, boss?"

The Manager nodded.

"He can't bear to think of her going to the knackers. We can make room for her, can't we?"

"Sure, boss," said the stableman. "What's one more among so many?"

And indeed there were a great many animals in the large, tree-shaded field in front of the Old Horses' Home. They were of all shapes and sizes, and all possible colours, and most of them were well past their prime. But amongst all the ancient ponies and horses were three giants who were, in fact, not old.

Captain and Ladybird were Shire horses, one black, one brown, and

both with white stockings. Herbert was a Suffolk Punch – a chestnut like all his kind. All three were in good health but there was no work for them to do – tractors had taken their places.

Far larger and heavier and stronger than the rest, Captain and Ladybird and Herbert looked down their great Roman noses at all the other horses in the place.

One afternoon, the three giants stood side by side under a sycamore tree, watching as a horsebox came up the drive.

"Another old crock, I suppose," said Captain.

"A broken-down nag, I expect," said Ladybird.

"Or a cow-hocked pony," said Herbert.

They moved with ponderous dignity towards the gate at the top corner of the field. Here the horsebox had stopped, and the stableman, who had come out to meet it, was opening the gate for it to reverse in.

Captain and Ladybird and Herbert watched as the tailgate was lowered. Then they shook their great heads in disgust as down it walked an old grey donkey.

"Good afternoon," she said. "My name is Jenny."

"It is not a good afternoon," said Captain.

"And as far as we are concerned," said Herbert, "your name is mud."

"You may not be aware," said Ladybird in the most patronizing of voices, "that this is a Home for horses."

"And not," said Captain, "for whatever sort of animal you may be."

"I think," said Herbert, blowing a snort of disgust through his large nostrils, "that it's an ass."

"Come away, boys," said Ladybird, "and leave the wretched creature. You don't know where it's been."

All three turned and walked majestically back to the shade of the sycamore tree.

Chapter Two

Jenny stood watching the three big horses sadly. She thought of all her friends left behind on the beach, and she stretched out her neck and gave a series of creaking, groaning heehaws – the loudest, most mournful noise imaginable.

Many of the other horses and ponies in the field looked up at this

sound, and one animal detached itself from the herd and came over to the donkey. It was a little old skewbald pony, bony and swaybacked, and it walked right up to Jenny and touched noses with her and said in a croaky voice, "Welcome."

"I don't think I am," Jenny said. "Those big horses were horrid to me."

"Don't take no notice," said the skewbald pony. "They'm like that, them three. My name's Alfie, by the way."

"I'm Jenny."

"Toffee-nosed lot they are," said Alfie, nodding his head towards the sycamore tree and the three huge rumps, one black, one brown, one chestnut, of Captain and Ladybird and Herbert. "And they're big-headed with it, not to mention the size of their backsides."

"They are rather fat," said Jenny.

"Fat as butter," said Alfie. "Just the job for the rustlers."

"What are they?"

"Horse-thieves. Chaps that do come round and nick horses."

"How do you know about these rustlers?" said Jenny.

"Heard tell about them from an old grey mare that used to live here. Dead now she is, but I can remember her telling me about these men that come round, at night usually, and steal livestock – cattle, sheep or horses. Once she saw a whole flock of sheep loaded

up into a lorry and driven away."

"But why would they want to steal those three big horses?"

"To ship 'em across the water. To France – it's not far. Be worth their while to come for those three great lumps of lard. Why, they must weigh nearly a tonne apiece," said Alfie.

"But what would they send them to France for?" asked Jenny.

"For meat," said Alfie. "Didn't you know they eat horses in France?"

Jenny let out another ear-shattering bray.

"Eat *horses*!" she said. "How dreadful!"

"Oh, I don't know," Alfie said. "After all, your Englishman eats beef and lamb and pork. It's just that he wouldn't think of eating horses. He'd sooner keep 'em in a Home like this, costing hundreds of pounds to be looked after. But your Frenchman, he's got more sense. He sees a nice fat horse and he thinks to himself, '*Ooh là là!* Horse-pie!' "

"Do the French eat donkeys?" Jenny said.

"I don't reckon so," Alfie said. "They wouldn't eat you, old girl, nor me, nor any of the old hat-racks round here. We'm all skin and bone. The rustlers wouldn't look at us, so don't worry your head about that."

But Jenny did worry. She was a kindly animal by nature, and the thought of the possible danger to Captain and Ladybird and Herbert upset her very much. Rude and overbearing they might be, but the idea of those magnificent creatures being stolen and taken away by lorry and then by ship to France, there to be killed and made into horse-pie – that was horrifying!

Chapter Three

For the rest of that day Jenny could think of nothing else as she grazed her way about the big field in Alfie's company.

Alfie, she noticed, though among the smallest of the ponies, was obviously a figure of some importance. He introduced her to the others as they met, and on the whole they greeted her in a friendly fashion. Though when a mare with a bit of breeding about her said, "An ass! What next?" she soon regretted it, for Alfie wheeled, quick as a cat, and his hind hooves beat a tattoo on her ribs.

But the three great carthorses were a different matter. One after another they worked their way close to the donkey and then, suddenly, lashed out or tried to bite her back. Once they lined up together and galloped across the field towards her, snorting and whinnying, as though they meant to squash her into the very ground.

"Let's hope the rustlers get you!" shouted Alfie as they dodged out of the way. "Horse-pie, that's all

you're good for!" But, of course, the thunder of hooves drowned his words.

"These rustlers," Jenny said. "When do they come?"

"At night," said Alfie. "Likely they'll have a big cattle-lorry parked down on the road, and then they'll come up the drive on foot, with halters."

"And how will they catch Captain and Ladybird and Herbert?"

"Sugar-lumps, I shouldn't wonder," said Alfie. "They'll go anywhere for a sugar-lump, they will. All the way to France, in fact."

"Alfie," said Jenny. "We must stop them."

"Stop who?"

"The rustlers."

"Whatever for, old girl? Good riddance to bad rubbish, I says. Nasty-tempered great things."

"I don't care about that," said Jenny. "They're still English horses and I'm an English donkey, and I'm not having them made into French horse-pies. We must stop the rustlers."

"Oh, nothing easier," said Alfie acidly. "You just waits by the gate and when the rustlers open it, you nips out and down the drive, and then you punctures all the tyres on the cattle-lorry."

"How do I do that?"

"Bite 'em."

For answer Jenny rolled back her lips, and Alfie could see that what few teeth she had left were blunt and brown and broken.

"Oh," he said. "Perhaps not."

"No," said Jenny, "but you've given me an idea."

"What?"

" 'When the rustlers open the gate,' you said."

"Well?"

"There's only one gate to this field. There's no other way for Captain and Ladybird and Herbert to be taken out. The post-and-rail fence is too high, even if they could be made to jump it."

"So?"

"We wait until the rustlers are in the field with their halters and their sugar-lumps, and then we block the gate."

"You're joking, old girl," said Alfie. "You and me, stood in the gateway, trying to stop the rustlers leading those three monsters through? We'd get killed."

"We might," said Jenny, "but we needn't be alone. All the other horses and ponies could help. The rustlers couldn't get through the whole herd."

The stableman, coming out to have a look round his horses, saw the

skewbald pony and the donkey standing nose to nose. The pony was nodding his head vigorously.

"You've got something there, Jenny," Alfie said. "But they'd drive us out of the way after a bit. We shall need help from the stableman. How're we going to get him up in the middle of the night?"

"That's easy," Jenny said. "You leave that bit to me."

Chapter Four

"It's a funny thing, boss," said the stableman to the Manager of the Home, some days later, "but those horses are acting ever so strange. Every evening at dusk they gather round the gateway, in a tight mass, and then after a bit they move away, but not too far away. It's almost as if they were practising something."

"All of them?" the Manager said. "They all do this?"

"Not Captain or Ladybird or Herbert," the stableman said. "They don't seem to be part of it."

"Beneath their dignity perhaps," the Manager said.

"I watched particularly last night," the stableman said, "and it's old Alfie and that donkey that seem to be the ringleaders. They go around from horse to horse, and then the whole lot move over to the gateway. It's since that donkey came."

"Funny," said the Manager, "but you've reminded me of something. There's talk of rustlers in the district."

"Taking horses?"

"Yes. For the French trade. Put a stout chain and padlock on that gate, will you? It's the only one into the field."

That evening, Jenny and Alfie watched as the stableman carried out his orders.

"That's all right then," Jenny said. "If the rustlers do come, they won't be able to get in."

"Be your age," said Alfie. "No, on second thoughts don't, you're old enough as it is. But they'll cut through that chain in a jiffy. They're professionals, these chaps, they know what to expect. Mark my words."

Alfie's words were marked a week later.

The evening parade of the herd around the gateway had just been dismissed, and only Alfie and Jenny still stood there in the dusk.

Suddenly Alfie put his muzzle against Jenny's long, hair-filled ear. "Look," he said softly.

They watched as a shadowy figure came walking up the drive. The man, they could see as he neared them, looked quite respectable – just an ordinary chap taking an evening stroll.

He stopped at the gate and leaned upon it, and looked about the darkening field. There was just enough light left to show, in their usual place beneath the sycamore, the three giant shapes.

"Watch," said Alfie as the man, after looking carefully around, put out a hand to examine the chain and padlock. Then he turned and went silently back.

"A rustler?" Jenny said.

"Looks like it. Haven't heard no lorry yet, it's too early."

"Shall we tell the others?" said Jenny. "We could always block the gateway to stop them getting in."

"No, no," said Alfie. "We wants them to come in and then we'll stop them getting out. Catch 'em red-handed. You go on down to the bottom by the road, old girl, and listen out for a lorry. Your ears are bigger than mine."

Chapter Five

Jenny was dozing by the rails when, around midnight, she heard a cattle-lorry approaching. It parked just outside the fence, on the grass verge of the road. Its lights were switched off and three men got out and very quietly lowered the tailboard.

Jenny made off up the field.

"Look at that old moke!" one of the men said. "She's a walking skeleton."

"Don't think we'll bother with her," said a second man.

"Wait till you see the heavy horses," the third man said. "Why, they must weigh nearly a tonne apiece. Come on now, let's get a move on. I've got the bolt-cutters."

It was a darkish night, and the rustlers did not notice that, by the time they reached the gate, all the horses and ponies were alert, watching. The bolt-cutters made short work of the chain, and the men opened the gate, came into the field, closed the gate again, and set off towards the sycamore tree with their halters and their sugar-lumps. Behind them, the herd closed silently in front of the gateway.

Minutes passed, and then the

horses saw the three rustlers making their way back towards the gate. Behind each man walked a giant haltered shape, mumbling a sugar-lump.

"Right," said Alfie. "Stand firm, everybody." At his words, the ancients closed ranks even more tightly. Some faced the enemy, their yellow old teeth ready to bite. Some turned tail, prepared to kick the living daylights out of the rustlers. All stood waiting, dogged and determined.

"Get out of the way," the rustlers called, as quietly as they could. "Get out of it, you pack of miserable old deadbeats."

No-one moved.

Then Alfie's shrill neigh rang out.

"Captain! Ladybird! Herbert!" he cried. "Run for it! They're taking you to France, to make you into horse-pie!" At his words the three whirled away, dragging the halter-ropes from the men's hands, and thundered off across the field.

"Now, Jenny!" called Alfie, and from inside the donkey's aged frame came those awful creaking, groaning heehaws, loud enough to wake the dead.

The stableman woke with a start.

"Listen!" he said to his wife. "The old donkey's braying, in the middle of the night. That's not

natural. Something's wrong. Dial nine-nine-nine for the police. I'll get my gun," and he jumped out of bed.

Out in the field, the rustlers stood undecided, swearing, but Alfie had not done with them yet.

"Charge!" he cried, and now the whole herd of horses set off, straight at the rustlers, who threw themselves wildly over the fence and ran madly down the drive, pursued by the stableman. On the road a police car drew up beside the cattle-lorry.

Chapter Six

Down on the beach at Easton-super-Mare, the donkeyman leaned against one of his charges, reading the local newspaper. Suddenly he called to his son.

"Hey, Sam!" he cried. "Look at this!"

DONKEY FOILS RUSTLERS –
DRAMA AT OLD HORSES' HOME

A warning from an old donkey led to the arrest of three horse-thieves who were attempting to steal stock from the Old Horses' Home. As luck would have it, the donkey chanced to bray loudly in the middle of the night and thus give the alarm. The police were able to intercept the rustlers, who will appear before local magistrates next week.

"That's got to be our old Jenny, Dad!" said Sam. "It must be. She's the only donkey in the place."

"Wonder how she knew they were rustlers," said the donkeyman. "What a funny thing."

"Funny thing," said the Manager of the Old Horses' Home to the stableman as they stood by the gate, a couple of days later. "The two Shires and the Suffolk Punch seem to have taken quite a fancy to that old donkey. They never went near her before except to rough her up."

"I know," said the stableman. "Look at them all now, boss, standing together under the sycamore tree, chummy as can be. It's almost as though they realized

that they owe their lives to her. But of course they couldn't possibly know that."

Just then they heard a snickering beside them, and turned to see the old skewbald pony, baring his yellow teeth in what looked like a grin.

"Hello, Alfie," said the stableman. "What are you laughing at?"

THE END

THE GUARD DOG

DICK KING-SMITH

Illustrated by Jocelyn Wild

YOUNG CORGI BOOKS

THE GUARD DOG

Chapter 1

There were six puppies in the window of the pet shop. People who know about dogs would have easily recognized their breeds. There was a Labrador, a springer spaniel, an Old

English sheepdog, a poodle and a pug.

But even the most expert dog-fancier couldn't have put a name to the sixth one. In fact, most of those who stopped to look in the pet shop window either didn't notice it (because it was so extremely small) or thought it was a rough-haired guinea-pig (which it resembled in size and shape) that had got into the wrong pen.

'What on earth is that?' the rest had said to one another when the sixth puppy was first put in with them. 'Looks like something the cat dragged in!' And they sniggered amongst themselves.

'I say!' said the Old English sheep-dog puppy loudly. 'What *are* you?'

The newcomer wagged a tail the length of a pencil-stub.

'I'm a dog,' it said in an extremely small voice.

The pug snorted.

'You could have fooled me,' said the poodle.

'Do you mean,' said the Labrador, 'that you're a dog, as opposed to a bitch?'

'Well, yes.'

'But what sort of dog?' asked the springer spaniel.

'How d'you mean, what sort?'

The pug snorted again, and then they all started barking questions.

'What breed are you?'

'What variety of dog?'

'Why are you so small?'

'Why are you so hairy?'

'Are you registered with the Kennel Club?'

'How many champions have you in your pedigree?'

'Pedigree?' said the sixth puppy. 'What's a pedigree?'

There was a stunned silence, broken at last by a positive volley of snorts.

'Pshaw!' said the pug. 'He's a mongrel!'

At that they all turned their backs and began to talk among themselves.

'I say!' said the Labrador. 'D'you know what I'm going to be when I grow up?'

'A gun-dog, I bet,' said the springer spaniel, 'like me. I'm going to be a gun-dog and go out with my master and bring back the pheasants he shoots.'

'No,' said the Labrador, 'as a matter of fact I'm not. I'm going to be a guide-dog for the blind. A much more worthwhile job.'

'No more worthwhile than mine,' said the Old English sheepdog. 'I'm going to work sheep. I'll be galloping about all over the countryside . . .'

'. . . getting filthy dirty,' interrupted the poodle, 'while I'm having my coat shampooed and specially trimmed and clipped, and a silk ribbon tied in my topknot. I'm going to be a show-dog and win masses of prizes.'

The pug snorted.

'What about you?' barked the others. 'You haven't said what you're going to be when you grow up.'

'I am going to be a lap-dog,' said the pug loftily. 'I shall be thoroughly spoiled and eat nothing but chicken and steak, and the only exercise I shall take will be to walk to my food-dish. Pshaw!'

'What about me?' said that extremely small voice. 'You haven't asked me what *I'm* going to be when I grow up.'

The Labrador yawned.

'Oh, all right,' it said. 'Tell us if you must.'

'I,' said the sixth puppy proudly, 'am going to be a guard-dog.'

At this the others began to roll helplessly about, yapping and yelping and snorting with glee.

'A guard-dog!' they cried.

'Mind your ankles, burglars!'

'He's not tall enough to reach their ankles!'

'If he did, those little teeth would only tickle them!'

'Perhaps his bark is worse than his bite!'

'It is!' said the sixth puppy. 'Listen!'

Then, out of his hairy little mouth came the most awful noise you can possibly imagine. It was a loud noise, a very very loud noise for such a tiny animal, but its volume was nothing like as awful as its tone.

Think of these sounds: chalk scraping on a blackboard, a wet finger squeaking on a window-pane, a hack-saw cutting through metal, rusty door-hinges creaking, an angry baby screaming, and throw in the horribly bubbly sound of someone with a really nasty cough. Mix them all up together and there you have the noise that the sixth puppy made.

It was a dreadful noise, a revolting

disgusting jarring vulgar noise, and it set all the creatures in the pet shop fluttering and scuttering about in panic. As for the other puppies, they bunched together as far away as they could get, their hackles raised, their lips wrinkled in loathing.

At last, after what seemed an age, the sixth puppy stopped. Head on one side, he wagged his pencil-stub tail.

'You see,' he said happily in his usual extremely small voice. 'I can make quite a rumpus when I really try.'

Chapter 2

'Nobody will buy him,' said the other puppies later. 'That's for sure.'

'What a racket!' said the sheepdog.

'It made me feel quite ill!' said the gun-dog.

'A really common noise!' said the guide-dog.

'Made by a really common animal!' said the show-dog.

'Pshaw!' said the lap-dog.

They all stared balefully at the guard-dog.

'The sooner he's sold, the better,' they said.

And that afternoon, he was.

Into the pet shop walked a tall lady with a face that looked as though it had a bad smell under its nose, and a small fat girl.

'I am looking for a puppy,' said the lady to the shopkeeper, 'for my daughter. I know nothing about dogs. Which of these would you recommend?'

All the puppies lolloped forward to the inner wire of the pen, whining and wagging and generally looking as irresistible as puppies do. All, that is, except the guard-dog. He sat alone, small and silent. He was not exactly

sulking – that was not in his nature – but he still felt very hurt.

'Nobody will buy him. That's for sure,' they had said.

He resigned himself to life in a pet shop.

The shopkeeper was busy explaining the various virtues of the five pedigree puppies when the fat child, who was standing, sucking her thumb, took it out with a plop.

She pointed at the guard-dog.

'Want that one,' she said.

'Oh, that's just a mongrel puppy, dear,' said the shopkeeper. 'I expect Mummy would prefer . . .'

'Want that one.'

'But, darling . . .'

The small fat girl stamped her small fat foot. She frowned horribly. She hunched her shoulders. With a movement that was as sudden as it was decisive, she jammed her thumb back in her small fat mouth.

'She wants that one,' said her mother.

By the end of that day, the guard-dog was feeling pretty pleased with life.

To be sure, there were things about his new owners that he did not quite understand. It seemed, for example, that simple pleasures like chewing carpets and the bottom edges of curtains drove the lady into what he considered a quite unreasonable rage, and as for the child, she was temperamental, he thought, to say the least.

Though at first she had seemed

willing to play with him, she soon began to complain that his teeth were too sharp or his claws too scratchy or his tongue too slobbery, and had made a ridiculous fuss over a doll which had sported a fine head of hair and was now bald.

Strange creatures, he thought that night when at last all was quiet, but I mustn't grumble. I'm warm and well-fed and this seems a very fine house for a guard-dog to guard. Which reminds me – it's time I was off on my rounds.

Ears cocked, nose a-quiver, he pattered off on a tour of the downstairs rooms.

His patrol over, he settled down in a basket in the kitchen. There was plain evidence that he had done his duty. In the centre of the drawing-room, for example, there was a fine white fleecy rug, and in the centre of the rug was a bright yellow pool. In other rooms there were other messes.

Comfortable now, the guard-dog closed his extremely small eyes. It had been a tiring day, and he was just drifting off to sleep when suddenly, outside the kitchen door, he heard a stealthy sound! He leaped to his feet.

Chapter 3

Afterwards the family could not understand why their cat would never again enter the house, but lived, timidly, in the garden shed. They did not know that its nerves had been shattered by the simple act of pressing against the cat-flap, something it had done every day of its life. This had resulted instantly in a noise that sounded to its horrified ears like a number of cats being scrunched up in a giant mincer. Upstairs, the fat child woke screaming, and soon her mother came rushing down those stairs and stepped in something unusual at the bottom.

Even then the guard-dog might still have had a house to guard (for it was difficult for them to believe that so little a creature was capable of making so ghastly a noise), if only he had kept his mouth shut the next morning.

But he stuck to his task, challenging everything that seemed to him a threat to the territory which it was his duty to protect. Quite early, at the sound of whistling and the chink of

bottles outside the door, he woke his owners once more. And no sooner had they taken the milk in than the postman knocked, and they actually saw the guard-dog in action.

Happily unaware of the effect of his voice upon the human ear, and mindful only of his role – to give warning of the approach of strangers – the guard-dog kept it up all morning.

The cleaning woman (who found a great deal of cleaning to do), the paper boy, the electricity man come to read the meter, and a door-to-door salesman were each in turn greeted by the dreadful medley of sounds that emerged, full blast, from the guard-dog's tiny throat. Last came a collector for the RSPCA, the rattle of whose tin inspired the guard-dog to his loudest, longest and most furious outburst.

'RSPCA?' screamed his distracted owner. 'What about a society for the

prevention of
cruelty to people?'
And at midday,
as she unscrewed
the Aspirin bottle,
she said to her
daughter, 'I'm
sorry, darling,
but I cannot
stand that row
a moment longer.
It'll have to go.
Will you be very
upset?'

The small fat girl, her eyes fixed malevolently upon the guard-dog, did not even bother to remove her thumb from her mouth. She merely shook her head, violently.

That afternoon the guard-dog found himself, to his surprise, in a very different kind of home – the Dogs' Home. He could not make out what had gone wrong. What were guard-dogs meant to do if not guard? He had only done his duty, but all he had received so far had been angry looks and angry words before finally they bundled him into their car, and drove him to a strange place full of strange dogs and left him.

26
27

From the kennel he had been given, Number 25, he looked round him. There was every sort of dog in the kennel block, young and old, handsome and ugly, large and small (though none remotely as small as he). Why were they all there?

'Why are we all here?' he asked the dog directly opposite him, a sad-looking animal with long droopy ears and a long droopy face.

'Because,' said the dog dolefully, 'we are all failures.'

I don't get it, thought the guard-dog. My job is to give warning of the approach of strangers. I've never yet failed in that.

'I don't think I'm a failure,' he said.

'Well, you're certainly not a success,' said the long-faced dog, 'or you wouldn't be here. All of us are here because our owners couldn't stand us any longer.'

'But we'll get new owners, won't we?'

'Possibly. It depends.'

'Depends on what?'

'On whether you take someone's fancy. You just have to do whatever you're best at. Me, I'm best at looking sad. Some people like that.'

In the days that followed, many people in search of a suitable pet came

to inspect the twenty or so current inmates of the Dogs' Home; and when they came to the end of the range of kennels and found the smallest inhabitant, they would without exception break into smiles at the

sight of such a charming little scrap.

Without exception, however, they were treated to the dreadful spectacle of the guard-dog doing what he was best at. And without exception the smiles vanished, to be replaced by

looks of horror as they turned away with their hands clapped to their ears.

By the time the guard-dog had been in the Dogs' Home for a week, most of the animals had gone happily

(or in the case of the long-faced dog, sadly) away with new owners, and there were newcomers in most of the kennels.

By the thirteenth day, there was only one dog left of those who had been there when he was admitted. This was his next-door neighbour, an old and rather smelly terrier.

The guard-dog's attempts to make conversation with it had always thus far been met with a surly growl, so he was quite surprised when he was suddenly addressed.

'You bin in 'ere thirteen days, littl'un, an't you?' said the terrier.

'Oh,' said the guard-dog, 'have I?'

'Ar. You come in day after I. 'Tis my fourteenth day.'

'Oh well,' said the guard-dog, 'try not to worry. I'm sure you'll soon be gone.'

'Ar,' said the terrier. 'I shall. To-day.'

'But how can you know that? How can you know that someone's going to take you away today?'

'Fourteen days is the limit, littl'un. They don't keep you no longer than that.'

'Why, what do they do with you then?'

'An't nobody told you?'

'No.'

'Ar well,' said the old terrier. ''Tis all right for us old uns, 'tis time to go. I shan't be sorry. You don't feel nothing, they do say. But 'tis a shame for a nipper like you.'

'I don't understand,' said the guard-dog. 'What are you trying to tell me?' But though he kept on asking, the old dog only growled at him, and then lay silent, staring blankly out of its kennel. Later, a man in a white coat came and led it gently away.

Chapter 4

'Oh, thanks,' said the manager of the Dogs' Home, when one of his kennelmaids brought in his cup of coffee at eleven o'clock next morning. He looked up from his record book.

'Shame about that little titchy one in Number twenty-five,' he said.

'You don't mean . . .?' said the kennelmaid.

''Fraid so. If things had been slack we could have kept him longer, but the way dogs are pouring in, we must keep to the two-week rule. He's one for the vet today.'

'Oh dear,' said the kennelmaid. 'He's such a lovely little fellow. Dozens of people fell for him, until . . .'

' . . . until he opened his mouth,' said the manager. 'I know. It's a pity, but you can't blame them. In all my long experience of every sort of dog, I've never come across one with such a dreadful voice. Nobody could possibly live with that; though, talk about burglar alarms – any burglar would run a mile if he heard that hullabaloo. And you wouldn't need to dial nine-nine-nine – they'd hear it at the nearest police station easy.'

The guard-dog ate a hearty breakfast, and was a little surprised when the kennelmaid came to clean out his run,

at the fuss she made of him. She cuddled and stroked and kissed him as if she would never see him again.

Then he remembered what the smelly old terrier had said. This is my fourteenth day, he thought. Great! Someone will pick me out today! He sat, waiting for the time when the public were admitted, determined that today of all days he would leave no-one in any doubt as to the quality of his greatest asset. Other guard-dogs, he supposed, might act in other ways, by looking large and fierce (which he could not) or by leaping up and planting their feet on the shoulders of burglars and suchlike and knocking them flat (which he

most certainly could not). He had only his voice, and when the door to the kennel block opened, he let rip, fortissimo.

No-one even got to smiling at him that morning. Everybody kept as far away as possible from the dreadful sounds issuing from Number 25, and concentrated upon the other inmates. The guard-dog was left strictly alone.

When at last the batch of would-be owners had left, some with new companions, some empty-handed, all mightily relieved to reach the comparative peace and quiet of the busy roaring street outside, the guard-dog sat silent once more. There was a puzzled look on his extremely small and hairy face.

Can't understand it, he thought. Nobody seems to want a decent guard-dog. But if fourteen days was the limit, then they'd jolly well have to find him somewhere to go today. Perhaps the man in the white coat would take him too – he'd seemed a nice sort of chap.

He watched the door to the kennel block.

It was not the man in the white coat who came in but the kennelmaid with a man with white hair, who walked with a stick with a rubber tip to it.

'Would you like me to come round with you?' the kennelmaid said, but

he did not answer, so she went away and left him alone.

The old man walked slowly along the row of kennels, looking carefully into each with sharp blue eyes. At last he came to Number 25.

Outside the door, the kennelmaid stood listening, her fingers tightly crossed. But then she heard that fearful noise start up and shook her head sadly.

She went back into the kennel block to find the old man squatting on his heels. There was a grin on his face as he looked, apparently totally unmoved, at the howling bawling yowling squalling guard-dog. He levered himself to his feet.

'I'll have this little fellow,' he said firmly. 'He's the boy for me.'

'Oh good!' cried the kennelmaid. 'He's lovely, don't you think?' But the old man did not answer.

He did not reply later either, when he had paid for the guard-dog and the kennelmaid said, 'Would you like a box to carry him in?' And in answer to the manager's question, 'What are

you going to call him?' he only said, 'Good afternoon.'

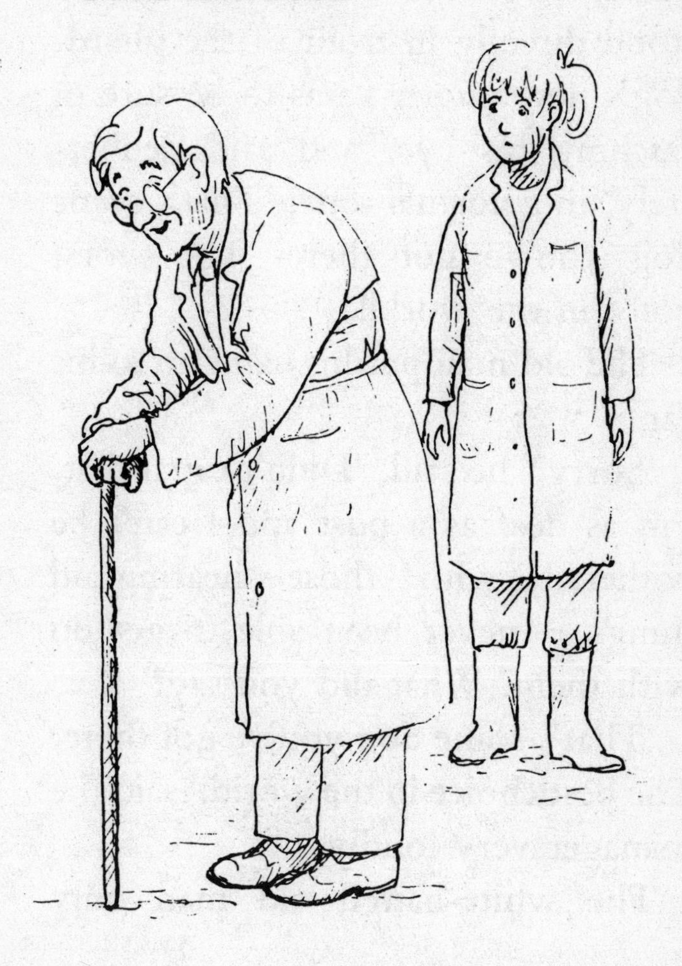

Light suddenly dawned on the manager of the Dogs' Home. He stood directly in front of the guard-dog's new owner so as to be sure of catching his eye, and said deliberately, in a normal tone, 'That's some dog you've got there. The worst voice in the world!'

The old man put his hand up to his ear.

'Sorry?' he said. 'Didn't catch that. I'm as deaf as a post and I can't be bothered with those hearing-aid things – never been able to get on with them. What did you say?'

'That's some dog you've got there. The best choice in the world!' said the manager very loudly.

The white-haired old man only

smiled, leaning on his stick with one hand and cradling his purchase in the other.

The manager shouted as loudly as he could, 'He's a dear little chappie!'

'See that he's really happy?' said the old man. 'Of course I will, you needn't worry about that. We'll be as happy as two peas in a pod.'

He fondled the puppy's extremely small hairy ears.

'Funny,' he said. 'I fell for him though he wasn't actually what I was looking for. I live all on my own, you see, so really it would have been more sensible to get a guard-dog.'

THE END

ABOUT THE AUTHOR

DICK KING-SMITH needs no introduction as the bestselling, award-winning author of *Harriet's Hare*, *The Guard Dog*, *The Sheep-Pig* (a box-office hit when released as the film *Babe*), and many other titles. He was voted Children's Author of the Year in 1992, won the 1995 Children's Book Award with *Harriet's Hare* and the Bronze Medal for the 6–8 age category of the 1996 Smarties Prize for *All Because of Jackson*.

Animals have played an important part in Dick King-Smith's life, ever since the days when he was a farmer in Gloucestershire, and many of his titles feature animals as the main characters. He gave up farming at the age of forty-five and later became a primary school teacher, teaching in a village school for a number of years. Now a full-time author, Dick King-Smith lives and works in a 17th century cottage near Bristol.

ALL BECAUSE OF JACKSON

by Dick King-Smith

'I want to sail the seas,' said Jackson.
'I want to see the world . . .'

Jackson is a very unusual rabbit – a rabbit with a dream. He spends his days watching the tall sailing-ships coming and going. He *longs* to go to sea, too. So one day – with his girlfriend, Bunny – Jackson stows away on the *Atalanta* and sails off in search of a new life . . .

A fascinating and funny tale from master storyteller Dick King-Smith.

'Dick King-Smith at his best . . . it stands reading and re-reading , and each time you chuckle at something different'
INDEPENDENT

YOUNG CORGI BOOKS

OMNIBOMBULATOR
by Dick King-Smith

'OUT OF THE WAY. TITCH!'

Omnibombulator is a very small beetle – so small that his parents give him a really long name to make him feel important.

It doesn't seem to help. Earwigs and woodlice still push poor Omnibombulator around, and snails walk across him, making him all slimy. Then, one day, Omnibombulator sets out to see the world – and discovers just how useful being really small can be . It all begins when he crawls into the toes of a huge old boot for the night, and a tramp with very smelly feet finds the boot . . .

From master storyteller, Dick King-Smith, bestselling author of the award-winning *Harriet's Hare*, *The Guard Dog* and *Horse Pie*.

0 552 52799 8

YOUNG CORGI BOOKS